BIG IDEA'S

Jonah
a VeggieTales Movie

the

Pirates

Who Don't Do Anything
usually

*To: Ben   On his 6th birthday
2002
From: Grandma & Grandpa*

Written by Eric Metaxas and Cindy Kenney

Illustrated by Ron Eddy and Robert Vann

Based on the movie: Jonah–a VeggieTales Movie

Written and Directed by Phil Vischer and Mike Nawrocki

BIG IDEA
BOOKS

Zonderkidz

www.bigidea.com

Zonder**kidz**™

The children's group of Zondervan

www.zonderkidz.com

Jonah and the Pirates Who Usually Don't Do Anything
Copyright © 2002 by Big Idea Productions, Inc.

Requests for information should be addressed to:
Zonderkidz: Grand Rapids, Michigan 49530

ISBN: 0-310-70460X

Written by: Eric Metaxas and Cindy Kenney
Editors: Cindy Kenney and Gwen Ellis
Cover and Interior Illustrations: Ron Eddy and Robert Vann
Cover Design and Art Direction: Karen Poth and Jody Langley
Interior Design: Ron Eddy

Library of Congress applied for

Printed in the United States
02 03 04 05/WP/5 4 3 2 1

To Mr. Twisty.
We sure do love
those twisted
cheese curls!

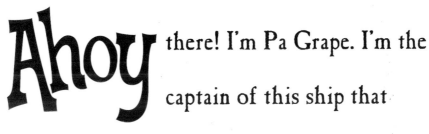**Ahoy** there! I'm Pa Grape. I'm the captain of this ship that doesn't go anywhere, and I want you to meet a couple of my friends, Larry the Cucumber and Mr. Lunt. We're the Pirates Who Don't Do Anything! And what that means is that we don't do anything! Nothing. Nada. Zip.

But to be completely honest, we really did do something once. Just once! I figured you might want to hear about it. It's a good story.

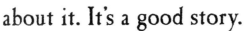

It was a very long time ago. We were hanging out down by the seashore not doing much of anything. Except for eating cheese curls. We love cheese curls. We love the way they go KA-RUNCH!

Anyway, this guy named Jonah showed up. He wanted us to take him to a faraway place called Tarshish! We told him, "No way!" After all, we're the Pirates Who Don't Do Anything!

Then he offered to pay us a whole mess of money. When we figured how many cheese curls we could buy, we knew we oughta think about it. Even though we're the Pirates Who Don't Do Anything, we love to eat cheese curls.

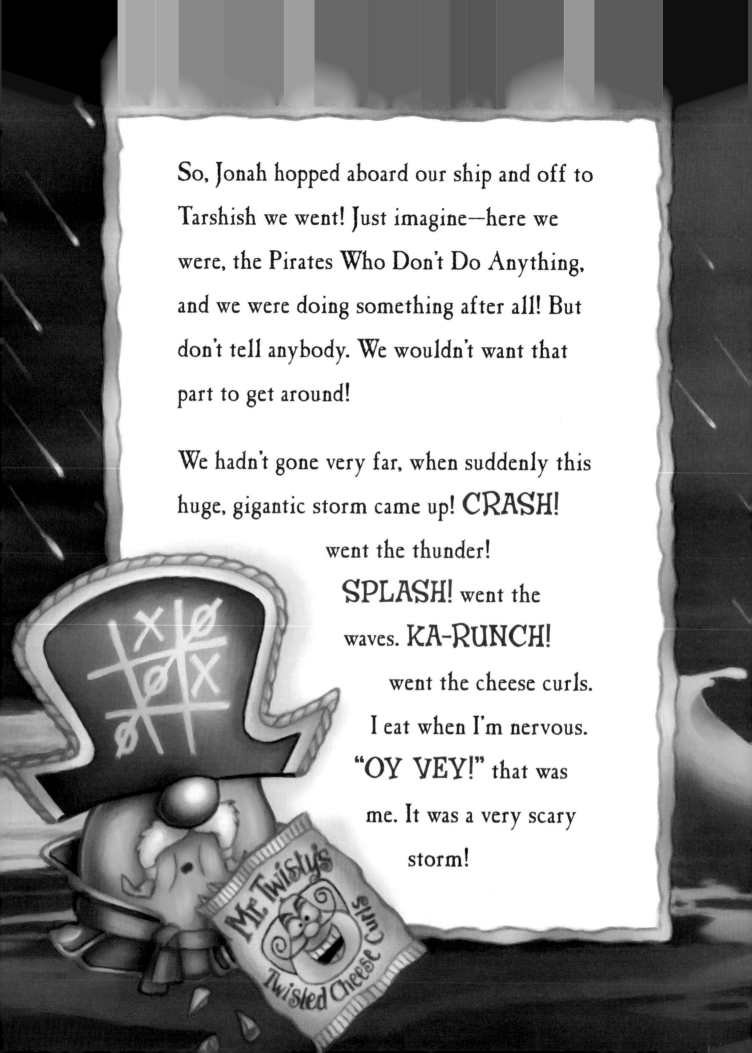

So, Jonah hopped aboard our ship and off to Tarshish we went! Just imagine—here we were, the Pirates Who Don't Do Anything, and we were doing something after all! But don't tell anybody. We wouldn't want that part to get around!

We hadn't gone very far, when suddenly this huge, gigantic storm came up! CRASH! went the thunder! SPLASH! went the waves. KA-RUNCH! went the cheese curls. I eat when I'm nervous. "OY VEY!" that was me. It was a very scary storm!

Anyway, we figured that somebody up there was pretty angry with somebody down here. And it was time to find out who it was. That's when I got this great idea. We could play a card game called "Go Fish." It's really fun.

So we played the game, but there was one rule. Whoever lost, walked the plank!

Everybody played the game, Larry, Mr. Lunt, and me, plus Jonah and this annoying worm named Khalil who sold stuff. I figured he was the troublemaker!

But you know what? I was wrong. It wasn't Khalil who lost the game. It was Jonah. And sure enough, Jonah confessed he was to blame for everything!

You see, Jonah was a prophet. That's a guy who gets messages from God and delivers them to others. God wanted Jonah to deliver a message to some people in Nineveh. But Jonah didn't listen. He ran away instead. That's because Jonah didn't like those Ninevites. They were really mean. They slapped each other with fish!

Have you ever been slapped with a fish? Oy! Does it sting! And it's all slimy!

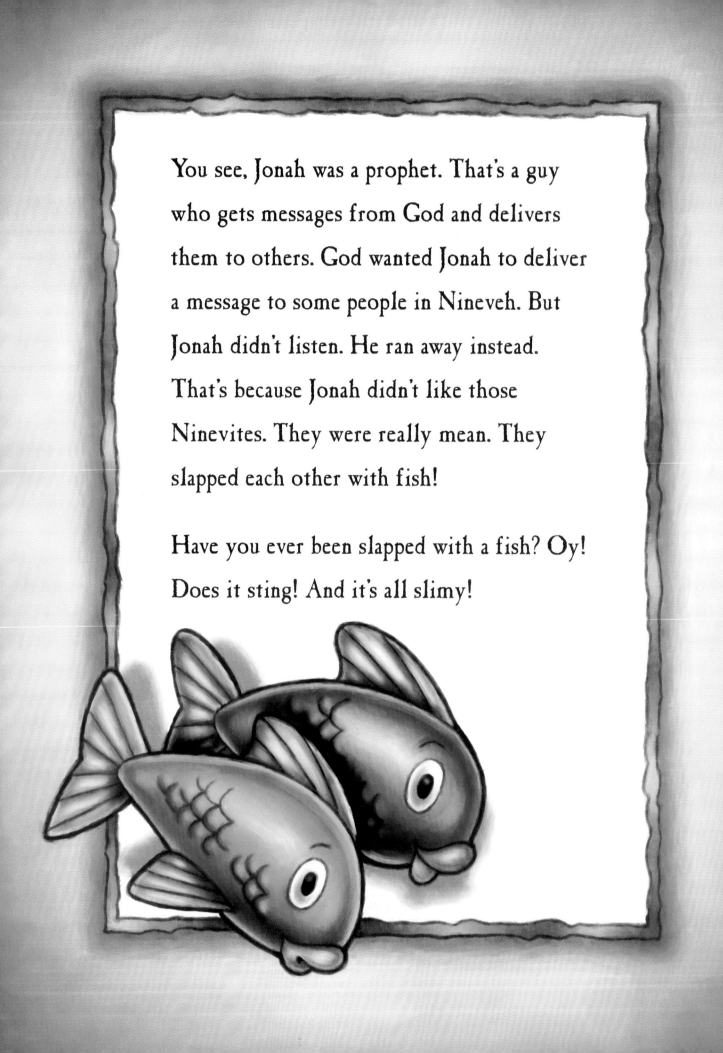

Anyway, Jonah didn't want to go there. That's why he ran away and jumped on board our ship. That's also why God sent a great big gigantic storm! So Jonah said if we tossed him overboard, God might keep the rest of us safe. But Larry told Jonah he didn't have to get tossed overboard. We had a plank he could just walk off! So he did.

KA-PLOOSH!

Sure enough, the storm stopped. It was a lot easier than anybody expected. So we tried to reel him back in. Larry tossed him a life preserver, and Jonah grabbed it.

That's when something amazing happened.
A big fish swam up and swallowed Jonah
whole! One big GULP! Just like that!

Then the fish started pulling us through the
water! So we started shooting stuff at him.
We loaded up the cannon with whatever we
could find.

"Fire one!" I shouted. KA-BOOM!
Out shot a tennis racket.
"Fire two!" KA-BOOM!
Out shot some croquet
mallets! Fire three!
KA-BOOM!
Out shot a
bowling ball.

The fish jumped up and swallowed the bowling ball! That was good for us, but not so good for Khalil. He was inside the ball.

Khalil said that the bowling ball rolled right up to Jonah inside the belly of that whale.

Khalil tried to cheer Jonah up, but old Jonah was being a real grumpy pants. Then all of a sudden they heard voices. Khalil said they heard some kind of musical number or something that told Jonah how God was a God of second chances!

So Jonah prayed and asked God for a second chance to go to Nineveh and deliver God's message.

And guess what happened! God gave him a second chance! BURRPPP! The big fish burped Jonah and Khalil right out of his mouth and onto the sand. And surprise! Jonah's camel, Reginald, was there waiting for him.

Jonah went to Nineveh and told those people, "STOP IT!" God didn't want them to keep slapping each other with fishes! God doesn't like it when people are mean. And you know what? They obeyed God's message. Even the king was sorry for acting that way.

So God gave the people in Nineveh a second chance, just like he gave Jonah a second chance!

You know, sometimes we all need second chances. I know I do. How about you? Have you ever needed a second chance for something?

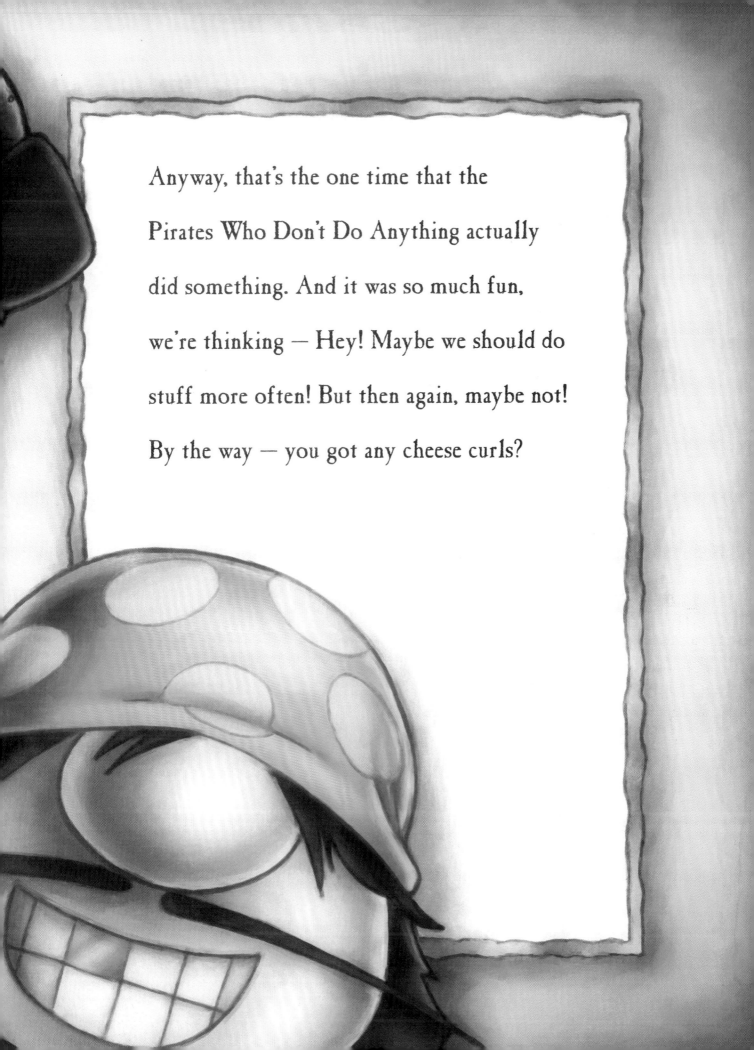

Anyway, that's the one time that the
Pirates Who Don't Do Anything actually
did something. And it was so much fun,
we're thinking — Hey! Maybe we should do
stuff more often! But then again, maybe not!
By the way — you got any cheese curls?